# You Stole My Shroom

Randi-Anne Dey

You Stole my Shroom



Published in Canada

Randi-Anne Dey Publishing

ISBN

978-1-0692484-7-3  Soft cover Book

978-1-0692484-8-0  ebook

# Dedication

*Dedicated to all those with friends that push you to step outside the box, or rather, into the mists.*

# THANKS

*Thanks to the crew*
*Deacon, Mags, Moo, Mythic*
*for the fun we had in the mists*

# Contents

# Disclaimer

*This book is written from a gamer's point of view while playing a MMO (Massive Multiplayer Online) where you become one with the character on the screen and it's as if you are actually there.*
*Enjoy the blending of reality and fantasy.*

*Gaming terms and their meanings are at the back of the book*

# The Players

*Mythicbubble - Dwarf Paladin Tank*

*Solstyx - Human Paladin Healer*

*Novena - Space Goat Paladin Damage*

*Catrionamoo -  Half dragon Hunter Melee*

*Elotarra - Gnome Hunter Ranged*

# Chapter One

# The Calling

Logging into the game, I stare at the robot standing on the screen, knowing it's a formidable challenge; enough so that I left my toon, Elotarra here, when I logged out last night to research the fight. Of course, what was planned, never happened and I didn't do my research. Shifting in my seat, I turn to my laptop and search for the best way to defeat it, especially if I want to keep my pet rating up. Maintaining my rank three position requires dedication, and I have been slacking lately. Too much time in the real world and not enough time in the game realm.

Did I want to risk the death of a pet? Not really, but I know the cost of being a pet battle master. The last one with a pet standing wins, and I intend for it to be mine. Besides, there are trainers that can bring them back to life and having done a lot of battles during my time in the game, I know where most of them are in the game. It's faster to fly my toon there, then wait for the time-gated resurrection of the pets.

Shifting back in my chair, I read through the page, looking through for the least complicated strategy. Simple is always better. Finding one I like, I turn back to my main computer, scrolling through my list of twenty-three hundred pets, trying to find the ones that the site recommends. It's not likely I won't have them, but there are some pets that have been out of my reach. One day, they will all be mine.

As I shift them around for battle, a message pings across my screen. Closing the list down, I flip over to the messages, reading one from a friend. Mythic! His character is Treefeared, and he is the best damn bear in the game. Last season, there was even this rumor that he was in the top five of the world. Now, I will never get as good as he is, being that I am a clicker, and he is a keyboard warrior, but I still strive to be as good as he is one day. We all need goals, right? And he is it for me.

"Elo, come play."

Wait, did that say Mythicbubble? Not Treefeared. I open my friends list and scroll down, stopping at his name. Yes, it definitely says Mythicbubble. A Pally? That's new. He's always on Treefeared, his druid. I mean always. Ever since I have known him, and it's been years, he's run the same character. Unlike other players that shift with the seasons, changing their main based on the stats of what's best at the moment.

An invitation from him flashes across my screen, waiting for me to accept or decline his offer.

I reach for my Coke and take a sip, pondering his change of character and the reason behind it. Not that it is hard to figure out. The creators of the game certainly favored paladins. Overpowered, topping the charts, while the rest of us poor schmucks struggle to even come close to them. Especially when we decide to stick to a class we favour, one usually near mid to low rankings. Not that it matters with Mythic. He excels at anything he plays. He's just that type of player.

I recall one time he joined us for our casual raid, one we run on Saturday nights. Our guild, Honors Light, welcomes all players that want to raid with us, from the casuals to the serious. It was the previous GM, Gwynevere's motto, *Everyone is welcome, no matter what.* We are casual, and fun, but I will admit, I do love it when the high rollers come to help us. We brought him in as a healer, because we were healer short that night, and he ended up out damaging most of the raiders that were actually spec'ed as damage dealers, or as the gamers call it, DPS.

Sighing softly, I look at the robot once more in front of my character, and the timer that taunts me. One that I suspect will be expired by the time I return to this quest, causing me to lose the precious leveling tokens he grants if I complete it. Tokens that keep me at realm rank three, with only Stokers and White ahead of me last I looked. While Stokers has a huge lead of over eleven hundred points, I am creeping up the backside of White with only three hundred and seventy-nine points between us.

Hmm, I have acquired new pets recently, I might be even closer. I flip back to my laptop, heading to the pet counter page where I update my pets. Well, well, well. It looks like White has transferred off my realm, making me second! Yes! Now my goal has shifted. First place, here I come, even if there are over a thousand points separating us.

Leaning forward, I type a message back to him. "What are we playing at?"

"We are heading into a nine mists. We need you."

I pan my screen out over the landscape from the cliff edge that my character is standing on next to Mr. Robot. Debating the time and whether I want to risk such a proposition. The carved stone town below me ignored, along with the grasslands reaching out to the ocean as I consider it. Lifting a piece of popcorn to my mouth, I munch on it. A nine. That's difficult. Especially now, after the squish. Granted, I knew mists well, having been there when it was active several seasons ago with both Elotarra, my hunter, and Solilque, my bear tank.

Mythic's message flashes once more on my screen, drawing me from my thoughts.

"Look Elo. You will get to see me play a pally. Something other than Treefeared. Now accept the invite so we can start."

That piques my interest. It's enough that I click accept. For as long as I have known Mythic, Tree's his main character, and he does it extremely well. A druid of all types; tank, healer and boom boom DPS. He's my go-to when I struggle with my druid tank, or need help, and he's always there with answers. Secretly, he's my bear idol, but don't tell him that, though I suspect he knows.

I suppose, now that I have accepted, I can compare them. Hell, I might even stand a chance of beating him on the damage meters with this new toon, especially if he is tanking. But then again, this is Mythic, so my odds are slim. I type back into the chat box. "Alright, I am in, but I am talking with Kay, so you need to invade this disco."

Seconds later, the pings of them entering the Discord voice chat sound into my headset. The team, together once more, having scattered over the week to do quests and other things in the wilds.

Elotarra, known as Elo, my gnome hunter with a bow

- Bounce and Downey - My favorite pony pets.

Mythicbubble. Mythic for short, on a brand new dwarven pally tank.

Solstyx, otherwise known as Deacon, our pally healer.

Novena, space goat, another pally and my old guild master, known as Mags.

Catrionamoo, a half-dragon hunter like Elo, but close-combat. Nicknamed Moo because all her characters have moo in them somewhere. Well, Moo doesn't actually join the voice right away, because she is streaming her adventures to others, but her spirit is there.

And so there it is. The ones brave enough to step through the mists into the wilds beyond. No longer the easy monsters of the open world. (Unless it involves the sleeping otters down south. Those things are nasty! They wake up cranky and the smack down is quicker than you can say, heals. Insta-death.) The casual wandering creatures you see while mining, or flower picking, are a thing of the past.

Now the monsters have a purpose, and that purpose is to destroy all those that step through the veil. It's kill or be killed and there is a number we have to kill to succeed. The counters linger in the back of our minds, taunting us with each success and failure. Add a clock to that and it's pretty much a recipe for disaster, but here we are.

I stare at the white swirling portal on my screen, bravely debating whether I want to do this, watching Mythic's character step through first and phase out. He's always been the bravest of our group, rising to the challenges placed before him, but that's what makes him a good tank. Mags and Moo follow, their toons disappearing as well. I pan my screen over to Deacon's character, hanging in the open world, facing the pretty glowing stone standing there.

Biting the bullet, I guide my character into the mist and step through, seriously debating staying out here with him. Suddenly questioning my decisions and wanting to return to the robot. The robot would definitely be the safer option, but perhaps not as fun.

Inside, the feel is different. On the right side of the screen, jagged rock walls reach skyward, following the hill downward and wrapping around out of sight. The tangled roots of a giant tree flank the left side, its ancient bark as tough as leather with a vine gate embedded at its base.

Panning the screen, I look around for the glowing font, a gnarled podium of wood and stone, seeing it standing in the same place it always is. One that beckons me to put the key in, but today, it's not mine. No, my key is to another one, where spiders run rampant and not one I desire to see at the moment.

Today, Deacon is the key master, and he hasn't braved the portal yet to join us. Still outside the mists. Smart pally. But honestly, he is probably off getting a drink or ice cream and either lost track of time or got lost on the way to the freezer. It is something he gets teased for all the time, especially on raid night when the six-minute break timer ends and he's not back yet. As I debate stepping back through the mist into the wilds, Mythic's voice sounds across the Discord.

"Do we have a flower picker?"

Slumping in my chair, I groan and press the control button, activating talk in Discord, further confirming that I cannot run away. "Damn. I'm a wielder and a flower picker. I can get the gates."

Moo chimes in as she pops into Discord. "Yes, Elo for the win."

Deep within the mists, there are certain gates that will react and open by those who love nature enough to pamper the surrounding flowers. Really, it's a skill you pick in the game, but that sounds better. Gates that allow us to bypass certain mobs of monsters, like the ones I am staring at down the hill.

Monsters, (or trash as we call them,) that have not recognized our characters being there because they are lower level than us at the moment. But they will. As soon as we click the key to start, they will power up to match our skill. Their radius of detection will expand, and then, all hell will break loose.

"Good-good. Deacon, where are you?" Mythic asks.

"Standing at the stone, waiting for all of you." Deacon replies.

"We are all inside."

I chuckle at his comment of standing at the stone, waiting. I understand completely. They are strange colors for rocks and have a glowing rune etched in them. Who wouldn't be mesmerized by the stones? I have even spent many hours standing at the stones with my toons, especially when the runes are purple. Purple is the best color, after all. My entire house is purple on the inside.

In the game, all the shiny purples distract me and pull me away from my quests. Back when they first made the treasures shiny purple, Tobin, another friend I played with, would ask why I was suddenly veering to the left, despite our destination being in a different direction. "Treasure!"

I always got one of two replies. "You are worse than a squirrel," or "I didn't even see that! How did you?"

"Puurrpplee!!!! It's the best color ever!"

Not this time though, and we need Deacon to join us in the mists. If Mythic suckered me into doing this, then he was obligated to as well. No backing out now. I pan my screen as Deacon strides through the portal, dressed in all his shiny plate armor. In fact, I realize suddenly, Mythic and Mags are plate wearers, too.

Great. I roll my eyes, grateful this isn't a Zoom meeting. That makes me and Moo the squishiest in scale-mail. Not that mail is bad, especially compared to leather wearers or the clothies; it just isn't as good as plate. It also means we were going to take more damage.

I smile at Deacon's toon, the large healer icon tied to his name, knowing we were going to give him a run for his money, testing his skills all the way through this dungeon. And if he's not up for it, I have my two guardian ponies. Shimmery white body coats with their manes and tails, a blend of blue and purple, matching the tufts covering their purple hooves. A violet horn rises from each of their foreheads. Upon their hooves and hidden within the fur, fires dance, adding extra damage when they attack on my behalf.

Well, it doesn't really, but I like to think it does. They are ponies to me; unicorns to others. Ones that I searched specifically for when a friend mentioned seeing purple ponies out in the wilds.

Deep into the woods, I traversed, scouring the areas before I found them running free. (I mean, yes, Google told me where they were, but it's like the old tales your parents and grandparents told. Back in my day, I walked miles to school, through twenty feet of snow... etcetera) So yes, back to I scoured the woods looking for them. What a glorious sight, seeing them run their path through the woods, while others stood grazing near lakes. It made me want them even more.

I remember watching the screen, seeing my toon land there with a bow slung across her back, as I decided which one of them I was going to tame. Scanning over my bars, I realized I didn't even have my tame spell on my bar. Great. After searching through my spell book, I dragged it over to the side where I could access it, then I dismissed my current pets. Dismounting my character, I approached them to within range of the spell and clicked my button.

Sending buckets of love out toward the digital horse. Tiny little hearts floated around my character and the ponies, as well as danced in my mind. They are gorgeous! There were ponies in the last expansion, but they were green and yellow. Ugh, yellow. The worst color ever. Granted, I still got them cause I love unicorns, but I ended up putting them in the stable and choosing other pets. Now it's ponies all the way, though I am considering a dragon. Especially since a red dragon holds my heart. If I could find a red one to tame in the game, I probably would.

But I digress, back to taming. I got them. I could envision my toon running her fingers through their manes, feeling the silky coat as she caresses them, and them nuzzling her gently, because of her being their friend. They are majestic and despite what other players might think, to me, they are the best darn pets in the game. Plus - they grant a casting speed to all players in your party! Bonus!

Afterwards, knowing there was a mount to match them, I stepped into the maze. A dangerous task for the monsters within it had a desire to yank everyone's soul from their body, over and over. Killing your character instantly. I needed to look for the purple lanterns that would guide me to the nasty sprite at the end that held my mount.

It was a tough fight back in the day and I recall having to kite that damn sprite around, but eventually I defeated it and took the mount as my prize. I burned through all my defensives and my healing pots to survive. Since then, I have run that maze close to fifty times, helping others achieve the mount as well. I am a pro now.

Hearing the whistle of a pet being summoned on my screen, I pan around, immediately noticing Moo calling forth a pony as well. It brings a smile to my lips, even though hers has a tan and gold mane, its colors closer to resembling the fire that dances around them. "Excellent choice Moo. I debated them, because well, fire ponies, but purple holds my heart, so they won out."

"Nice, nice. I am going for the red and black one next."

"Yes, I tried back in the day, but they never spawned for me. I spent hours camping them and eventually I gave up. I mean, red and black would be cool, but purple is better. Though at the time, these didn't exist, so I was running blue rune carved dogs."

"You just need a dead realm. A lot of those rare monsters are up on those," Mags answers.

I laugh, knowing that's exactly where my toon is. "I am in a dead realm, Mags. When you all invite me to yours, there are far more people in town than I have, then they all disappear when we break the group. Either way, I have purple ponies now and they are the best pets to run with! They got a horn to stabby-stabby with. Hooves to stompy-stompy with, and magic to make us faster at casting and shooting. Who doesn't love being faster at things?"

"Yes, they are," Moo agrees.

"Is everyone ready?" Mythic asks.

"No," I reply, knowing Mythic has clearly grown tired of our chit chat. Despite my answer, he initiates a ready check and Deacon's toon moves over to the font to drop his key into it.

# Chapter Two

# Start Timer

My shoulders tense as I feel the stress meter in my body rise, causing my chair to rock back and forth as I fidget with nervous energy. I chew on my lips as I rub my hands together, trying to calm the nerves running rampant. It's not like I don't know this place. I have done it many times back in the past; it's just nerve wracking.

Don't get me wrong, I enjoy doing these once they start, but there is still the pressure on me to pull my own weight and beat Mythic on the damage meters. Especially since he's a tank and technically is not supposed to do as much damage as we do. I know my class, and I think I do pretty well at it, but not as well as others.

Lights flash on the screen as an ominous voice sounds from the monitor, counting down from three, ending in the screen flashing to a loading screen and the quiet click of the clock starting. Shifting the mouse over, I hit my call pets button and run my toon over to the first gate. Spending the time to click the cog-wheel over to open so that the group may skip the monsters at the bottom of the hill.

Mythic's character bolts down the hill, hugging tight to the tree root to avoid the monsters on our left, charging head first into the mobs at the bottom, followed by the rest of us. A tall tree-like dryad stands in the center, its leaves wilted and its wood bark tinged with shadows of black. Creatures that seem to be a mix between a satyr and a centaur surround it. Dark brown fur with glowing red eyes, and leather armor strapped across their chest. Each of them carries a bow which they wield with such a finesse that it never misses its target.

Gangly black creatures bounce around like they have springs in their legs as Mythic tries to round them up. I grimace as I watch my character's health plummet from them, landing on her, knowing this is exactly why this place is more dangerous than the wilds. Frantically, I try to find my healing button and dropping some shields around me. At least out in the wilds, the monsters actually can miss you.

Since I am ranged, I keep my character back, and out of melee. I don't really like being there anyhow unless I am a tank, because a lot of damaging spells end up there. Now my friends, they all prefer to get into the thick of things, but it's a bit too crazy for my desires. Clicking a few buttons, I command my ponies to attack while sending an array of arrows into the group. The black jumpers leap out to my toon, clearly shredding her again with the way my health pool dropped. Ye'ouch.

"Damn, those things hurt." I forgot that those nasty-ass creatures jump specifically to those of us that are ranged. Muttering under my breath, I scan through my bars and find a spell that will keep them contained, binding them in place and away from me, watching Deacon's healing magic pull my health pool back up. Yep, he's going to be working it hard in this dungeon.

Next I place a trap spell in front of my toon, something I do a lot of because it stops any charging creature from reaching me. A little trick another hunter taught me years ago, and I teach to others now. "Take that, you little cretins." Seeing them jump again, I watch them get yanked back, while another does actually get lodged in the trap. "Hah. I won this round."

Shaking my head, I pan the screen back to the fight, seeing Moo's toon pinned in much the same way. Encased in bark with enough vines wrapping around her that she looks just like a bonsai tree. "Moo! Nooo!" Knowing that is unacceptable, I turn my focus to the plants surrounding my friend and target all my attacks on them.

My ponies follow, because I have them macro'ed to obey my commands, using their hooves to pound the plants off her, trying to remember if the damage transfers to her as well. I recall that some effects in this game do, but I don't think this one does. I will admit, I breathe a sigh of relief when Moo's toon becomes free of its entanglement and jumps back in the fray. Yes, it's a game, but it's also more than a game. It's us against them and we need to win.

Shifting my toon closer, a crackling black beam strikes her. I immediately race Elo out of the breath weapon, or whatever it is, watching my health pool plummet. Darn it, I forgot about that too. Knowing my heal spells are not ready, I slam my control button down.

"Deacon!"

"I got you Elo."

Once Deacon has her stable again, I adjust my toon over to a clear spot, very much aware of the monsters on my backside, and not wanting to aggro them. A thin silver beam strikes my character, and I recall it's the one that wraps our characters up in roots.

No problem. This is where hunters excel. We can shrug a lot of effects off with our play dead abilities. Apparently, it tricks the creatures, and the death effect is pretty darn cute. My gnome jumps up and dramatically waves her hands before she grasps her throat, then collapses to the ground with a strangled cry. "Arrguagg."

I even went out and bought the play dead feat for my pets. They let out a whinny and flop over to the side. It's not as entertaining as my gnome, but it always makes me laugh; it's better than when I just let them die because I don't pay attention to their health bar. And that happens a lot. Enough so that my friends tease me that my ponies are going to abandon ship one day and run away from my poor treatment of them.

Once the beam is off, I wake my character up and continue with the fight. I can just imagine, if these were actual monsters and not computer generated, the creature's confused expression of how the gnome died, then returned to life. Pretty certain my gnome would call them out, for falling for the oldest trick in the book.

We finish the group off, freeing the tree and continue down the slope, while hugging the rock wall that's there. Before us lies a pool of water. "Great." I mutter under my breath about it, mentally trying to remember if this is a wading pool or a swimming pool.

Downside to playing a gnome. While other races walk through it, my character is often left swimming because of her short statue. Gnomes barely reach the knees of most of the other races in this game.

Upside? It won't affect her adorable yeti outfits. Could you imagine if the game ever added that? Slowed speed from waterlogged fun-fur. The large plush slippers she wears would slop around and add penalties as well. Then there is the drying time on that, let alone the cost to fix the rips and tears. There is already a gold cost for damage, but it doesn't show on the actual character, just behind the scenes.

To the right, against the rock wall that our characters are running beside, is a large marker with a swirling green symbol, sitting in what looks like red hex markings. To the left, the wall across from them appears to open up into a lake, surrounded by lush green grass and a blend of wildflowers.

Mythic's toon pauses momentarily as his voice comes through the Discord. "Do you guys know about the play-dead trick?"

If the toons could look at each other, I am sure Moo and Elo would. Hell, if we were sitting in the same room, I am certain we would share a look. Especially since the silence that follows in the Discord at the question clearly implies neither of us did.

My mind races. How did I not know about this? I know about the rogue one, where they can shroud us past the mob. Or the warlock one, where they drop a gate over the rock wall to the other side, stepping us past the mob. I can click a spell much like the rogue, blending into my surroundings and slipping past, but that's not tied to the play dead he is asking about. "Wait, what play-dead trick? I thought I knew them all."

I could feel Moo shrugging her shoulders through the Discord. "Not me."

"Never mind," he replies as he charges into the pack of five monsters.

I skirt my toon around the water, because well, it's easier to walk on ground and fight, than swim and fight. My mind is still curious as to what this trick Moo and I are supposed to know about and make a mental note to ask Mythic later. Tabbing through the newest pack, I decide to target the creature resembling an oversized baboon. It is made of dark wood, and is almost black if the right light hits it.

After sending my pets in, he retaliates and drops a black pool of sludge under my toon. My screen beeps, informing me of the incoming damage, just as my health drops. Shifting my character to the left, I send a barrage of arrows into the group, only to have to move away because more black sludge appears.

Right, avoid acid sludge. I forgot how often that creature casts that spell and the fact that he can drop that spell beneath the water and still have it affect our characters. Game mechanics... Ugh, I adjust my character yet again, really glad that I am not a caster that relies on standing still. This pack needs to drop fast. Cooldown time I guess. Gliding my mouse over my screen, I click the ones that burst damage, watching as more pets appear and dots flood through the mobs.

My addon pings an alert. Somewhere in the mob, someone is healing. Great. I am still attacking the baboon. Hopefully, the others can get it cause there is no way I can tab through and find it in time. In this game, you pretty much need to be targeting that specific monster in order to interrupt their spells.

Besides, my interrupting cast is so long at thirty seconds compared to others which range between ten and twelve seconds. It makes me pretty much useless once I use it. As soon as the baboon drops, I tab through to the caster, finding her just as she casts her heal again. Hah! I got this! I click my interrupt, only to see an addon flash on my screen that Moo has interrupted the cast. Well, that was a waste of my spell.

What seems like forever, with Mythic kiting the mobs around and Deacon trying to keep us alive from all the damage they are doing, they finally die. In this place, there are two packs that I recall us wanting to avoid if you can. This one, and one in the maze. But only if the faerie makes you turn left at the beginning. Let's hope that is not the case. Now this one is not as bad as the maze pack because that pack always decimates my tank, no matter what I do, and I have seen it decimate other tanks. It really needs some fine tuning.

Panning my screen to the left, I look out over the lake. This game really has beautiful scenery, even if pretty much everything wants to kill us. On that note, I notice the mobs on the other side appear to be friendly. It makes me wonder if the creators of the game made it so that the murder hobo mobs could not swim. An interesting thought really and one I might even try out, but not on a nine. Not that my toon can swim. She would be dead before she even made it halfway across. I would need to summon a water walking mount or the raft in order to outpace them and you can't do that in combat.

Realizing that Mythic is already advancing, I shift my screen and set my toon to follow him. I lift my gaze to my health, watching as Deacon weaves his healing magic upon us. Mythic marks the path he wants us to go. Wait, this is new. Usually we barrel into those four mobs right before the boss room. Moving my character to the path, I mutter softly to myself about having short legs and not being fast like the tall folk are.

Mythic stops his toon just before the stone wall. "We are going to hug this rock and the gate so that we can go around this group. They have casters that can be a bit of a bear."

I laugh, pressing my Discord button. "Funny… That comes from someone that plays a bear tank normally."

"You do as well Elo!"

"I know. That's why it's funny."

I shift my toon up and creep forward with my arrow keys because this kind of navigating makes it a touch more difficult with my mouse. Each of us with every intention of passing, but clearly the range of the mobs has changed. One of them turns towards us and casts, while the other two charge us.

Deacon chuckles. "No sneaking past them for us."

"Clearly not. It's gotta be the full-plate armor you are wearing 'cause I am dressed in a cute little onesie. Plate jangles, you know. You get negatives on your move silently checks."

"It was you Elo. I saw the arrow fly into the pack!"

"Was not!"

"Pew-pew, you two!" I am pretty certain I heard Mythic sigh through the Discord. Although it is far better than *'Danger-Danger.'* You *know* you are in trouble if Mythic is saying that and you better prepare to run with your toon if you hope to survive. Been there, done that. Ran all the way back to where the resurrection point was, using whatever I could to survive, dragging all the mobs with me, hoping the tank could round them up again.

"Hey! Only I pew-pews. Deacon healy-healy's."

"Which neither of you is doing!" Mythic's toon steps in between us and them, grabbing the two that charged forward and drags them back into casters, sending out his hammer to interrupt them.

"Right, I can talk and shoot." I mutter under my breath into the voice chat, feeling a little like a child being scolded for not doing her chores. Hey, I was sneaking just fine. I was even close enough to open the gate we were walking past. At least Mythic is quick at rounding them up and dragging them back to the casters before they can do any actual damage, so Deacon has a bit of a break.

"I can hear those thoughts Elo!" Mythic says.

"No, you can't"

Kay, who I was originally in Discord with, chuckles. "Even I can hear them Elo."

"You guys!"

Mags laughs. "Elo, you set yourself up so well."

"You all just pick on me cause I play a gnome."

"That's right!"

"You are all so bad!" Sighing, I shift in my seat at their teasing, clicking a few buttons and quickly grab a sip of my Coke. This pack is not so bad, though the two casters can cast heals, and that's who I set my focus to.

Seeing the one start, I place my Coke back and send an interrupt spell its way, only to hear my addon telling me the second one is casting. Great, I don't have one for that. "The other healer is casting!"

"I got it!"

"Perfect. No healing friends allowed."

Deacon chuckles, "I guess that makes my job here easier."

"I don't mean you, Deacon."

"Oh, so you are giving me permission to heal the bad guys?"

"No, I am not! Only heal us! Especially with the amount of damage these things are doing."

"Hey, I have healing, being a pally myself," Mags answers.

"I know Mags. You, Mythic and Deacon all have a decent amount of healing spells. Moo and I have one and a potion if we remember to buy them in town."

"Yo. Don't worry Elo. I got you. I won't let you die!"

"That's good. If you do, it counts as time against us!"

# CHAPTER THREE

# SHROOM GATE

I look over the bodies that lie at our characters' feet, knowing we have more to go through. Turning my toon to face the gate behind her, I move my mouse across the screen, searching for the cog-wheel. Finding it, I click on it and watch as the gate fades away, opening to a large clearing surrounded by sheer rock walls.

To the left, a cave entrance slopes downward, its dark mouth hinting at the descent within, and the monsters likely hiding in its depths. Scattered throughout the glade are clusters of red and purple mushrooms, mingled with patches of grass and wildflowers. They line rings of bare earth that spiral outward from the center, forming an unnatural pattern throughout the glade. "Don't forget to thank the plants for allowing us access."

"You really are one with nature, Elo," Moo teases.

"Nah, I am allergic to it. It likes to torture me. I like nature in games like this one! No pollen, no reactions."

"Gotcha. I get that."

"Yes, aloe juice for the win, otherwise my eyes would be puffy and swollen shut. That definitely limits my ability to see. No pew-pews for me. No writing. Just lying on a bed with tea bags over my eyes, hoping they return to normal."

"What about antihistamines?"

"No can do. Bad kidneys and the kidney meds react with them. No nsaids either, like muscle relaxants. Just plain old Tylenol if I am suffering. To add to that, I can't even have grapefruit! It also reacts with my meds, which sucks cause I love them."

"That sucks."

"Yes, it does. Hence drinking aloe juice. A customer told me about it, and I didn't believe her. Then I tried it and it made about 80% difference in my allergies. That and sticking to picking flowers in a video game." I pan the glade. It's the mushrooms I am after. Ones that give us all an advantage if eaten. The purple ones are the best, but red would do if we are in a pinch. "Shroom room is open!"

Knowing time is ticking, I run my toon over to the first purple mushroom patch because usually the tanks go for the red ones, only to see Deacon's toon fly past me and sit in the patch, munching down on them. "Deacon! You stole my shroom!"

"Nom Nom." Deacon just looks up and continues to eat, as if a gnome tapping her foot at him was nothing to be concerned about.

"Arg! So not fair." Knowing if the characters in the game could taunt each other, Deacon's would look up, arch a brow and stuff another shroom in his mouth. Clearly ignoring my character, who would have her hands on her hips, tapping her foot. "My character has short legs! Longer legs go to the ones further out." I run her over to the next patch, finding Moo just sitting down, plucking a mushroom from the grass, and munching at it.

"Seriously? Moo! You too?"

"Hey! They are tasty!"

"I am sure they are, if I can get to one."

Scanning the clearing, I spot another patch on the far side. As my toon is running to them, Mags bolts past on her pally pony, racing over to it. "Damn, you all stole my shrooms!"

I know Mythic is already fighting at the sound of combat coming from my monitor, and I feel panic set in. Frantically glancing around, I spot a patch tucked up against the wall just beyond the cave entrance. Clicking on my speed burst, I run my toon over and settle her in the mushroom patch, watching the timer tick down as I eat. Once the food buff appears, I stand her up and pause, the glint of red drawing my attention.

Shinies always do in the game. I adjust the screen, angling it down into the cave, noticing a pack of mobs down there. I don't remember that and yet, here they are, patting around in the darkness. Shifting my character further away from the entrance, I race her back to the boss-room, watching Mythic's health drop drastically.

"Shit, that's not good. Deacon! Mythic is getting trounced."

"I'm fine. I have defensives." Mythic replies.

Arriving back at the battle with the others, I notice a ton of black sludge on the ground, with Mythic's character kiting the two black baboons out along the rock wall. Right, these are the ones that toss that crap every two seconds. "Right." I roll my eyes. "Defensives… And yet, you are at half your health."

"Ah, I just got hit by them and two sludges at the same time. I will be fine."

"Yo, I got you!" A golden aura surrounds Mythic as Deacon channels his healing into him.

Charging my character in, I send my ponies into attack, clicking my spells. Watching my timers, I shift just before the sludge drops, which, in essence, means my character is shooting and running at the same time. True hunter fashion and a perk of being ranged. I can stay out of it better, whereas Mags and Moo rely on Mythic moving the monsters and keeping them out of the toxic waste. "Good thing I am a hunter and not a mage, or this would suck."

"We are fine!" Mythic states.

"No stress. I got you," Deacon's magic wraps around our characters.

I watch our health bars climb slowly. I will admit, I tried healing once. NOT for me. I recall the characters taking far more damage than my healing spells granted. Huge respect for healers, which is why I am on it with avoiding damage. That and my class is a healer's nightmare, or so I have heard. (Looking at you, Mags!) I continue shifting around the battlefield, grateful when the first monster drops. Once the second one drops, I see Deacon's toon doing circles around mine.

"Look Elo, I have more shrooms!"

"You do not!"

"True! But if I could, I would have my character wave them just over your head, just to see you jump for them."

Mags laughs, "that would be funny to see."

"All of you! Stealing my shrooms. I had to run to the far side to get them! And if you did, I probably *would* jump for them."

"You know it! I would pick them all, and be buffed for the entire run if I could. In fact, I might just have to pretend I have done just that!" He chuckles.

"So not fair. I will get you back, Deacon, just you wait."

"I am counting on it. In fact, you should write a book about it!"

"I just might. Telling everyone what an evil healer you are, stealing my shrooms all the way through this place."

"I can see you doing that."

"Yep, all the blame will fall on you. Even if it doesn't."

"Shouldn't we roll for that?"

"Nope. It's all Deacon's fault."

"In that case, we should go to the junkyard next. I will entice the robots to run you over, too."

"Why?"

"Cause you are a gnome! Gnomes deserve what they deserve."

"I like being a gnome, and I am cute. Whenever I am in the city, I get whispers all the time telling me just how adorable I am."

"They clearly have no taste!"

"Yes, they do. They love me."

"You are still a gnome."

"Deacon! Why do you hate gnomies sooo much?"

"Just because."

"Fine..." I muttered, knowing they were teasing, but still fun to pretend I was sulking at their antics. We all know each other far too well. Even in raids, they torment my gnome character, using toys to change her into anything other than a gnome, though there are a few that steal her appearance. Yeti outfit for the win. They also mark her so that they can run effects over her, trying to kill her, but as I stated before, I am good at avoiding things. Some actually succeed, and while it's never said out loud, I bet there is gold transferred when they do. "We will finish this discussion later."

Hearing my screen beep, I realize my thoughts distracted me enough to miss the fact that there is sludge beneath my character's feet. My health plummets as I jolt the mouse to move her. "Damn, these monsters are brutal."

"Well, their sludge is."

"True that."

"I wish we still had acid arrows. Then two could play with acid to make it fair."

Mags laughs, "I just want the spells the monsters are throwing out."

"YES! Me too! Though some of them are not as strong as they seem when you look at the damage meters. Or even having the game react to your voice. Like egging on my pets to get them to fight better rather than pushing buttons."

"Can you imagine?"

"It would be amazing. There is normal talk here in disco, then there would be the behind-the-scenes talk where I would taunt my pets... Come on Bounce, Downey, you call those hits? I have seen you stomp better than that. Even my arrows are doing more than you, and they are teeny-weeny little sticks. And why aren't you using your horn to gore?! It's the best feature of being a unicorn!"

"Perhaps a virtual reality game?"

"Perhaps."

# Chapter Four

# Boss One

I watch the last mob die and quickly open my character screen, checking the damage on my gear, needing to know if I have to repair it before facing the first boss that is now standing before us. While the others do the same, I take a swig of my Coke, knowing a boss fight will keep us busy.

Panning around the room quickly, I smile at the rock walls, tall and sheer. Well over my character's head, but then everything usually is. Where others could walk or jump things, I have to do small hops to do the same thing, and often fail, earning their chuckles at my attempts. Though there are times I can fit in caves, or walk beneath things that they have to go around. That's always fun.

Especially when you convince a guildie to come out to this remote island. Showing her all the things it offered. I ran into one cave as she was trying to follow. Then I clicked a spell that switched our locations magically, sealing her in a cave. She couldn't get out because she was too tall, and I could freely walk in and torment her. Eventually, I switched her back, and I am pretty certain she never trusted me again.

Not that they don't torment me like that.

There was another place. Down in the under-dark where Kay and I were exploring. We do that a lot. I mean, the game wouldn't offer these places if they had not intended for them to be explored. Right? There was a lovely set of wrought-iron gates. Behind it, you could see monsters, and that meant treasure. It also helped that there was a treasure box on my map, not too far from the gates.

We figured out a way up the rock wall and jumped over. My character was dead before I even hit the ground. So was Kay's. Now, he managed to get his body back and return to safety, but I was too far in there to do so. I could get to my body as a ghost, but the second I rezzed, I insta-died. I even tried to shield and hearth home, but I died too fast to get the cast off. Ah, exploration of unknown territories. Did I learn from it? No. Do I still explore? Hell ya.

Blending into the walls is a large willow tree with branches hanging over our characters' heads. Its roots spread out across the floor; ones that are a tripping hazard for the others but a full climbing hazard for me because of my toon's short legs. Every so often, there is the brief flicker in my mind to play something other than a gnome, like my friend Kay does, one who can jump and glide over things. When I say brief, I mean it. No longer it then a few seconds. Not that I don't have my bear tank, Solilque or my mage Caranip, but hunter holds my heart with my tank a close second. Cara is up there because she was the first character I ever created in the game.

Dark blue runes lie scattered upon the floor, blending with the same dirt spiral and wild flowers that the shroom room has. On the left, they rise and curl over another gate. Unlike the last two, where vines held them closed, this one has a blue swirling mist filled with purple flickering lights.

Hanging above it, dangling from the roots, are lanterns, glowing a soft orange and red, with one purple dangling in between them. This place really is beautiful, even if it's deadly.

Turning my attention back to the middle, I focus on the two creatures waiting there. Another one of those tall gangly trees, wrapped and entwined with a black spell, just like the very first one. Beside him, a shorter, but still taller than the others, satyr-ish creature. Both of them are standing on the dark runes, etched into the dirt and glowing with a blend of light and dark blue, probably enhancing them, which would not be good.

There was a manor that had the same runes and it's the tank's job to drag them off them, otherwise all the mobs either healed or were power boosted. Granted, some would not move unless you interrupted their spell-casting, and that was usually on us, and not the tank. I love the classes that have the spells to drag their enemies to them or knock them off it like my bear. They are the best.

I mentally wrack my brain, trying to recall their skills and abilities. It has been years since I have been in here, and I know they have changed some things for this season. No charges that I could recall, so being ranged is fine. Green puddles of death that spawn all over the room. Check. Something that needs interrupting, but damned if I can remember what. "Any changes I should be aware of?"

"Not that we know of," Moo answers.

"K, good."

Without commenting, Mythic charges into the fray, going straight to the dude. About to target the same one, I remember at the last second, that we need to burn the shield off the tree-dude. Right. Tabbing over to him, I mark him and tap all my big spells, sending a variety of pets into the battle, as well as all my dots, before slipping into rotation. Focusing on this one because one wrong move and the boss will one-shot your toon.

Hearing my screen ping, I glance to my timeline addon. Green circles incoming. I sidestep them and back away from the boss, thinking there is far more than I remember spawning. The floor is practically green from all the sludge.

"Elo. You are out of my healing range!"

"Sorry Deacon, the green forced me back. I need to circle around it."

"See that you do. Your health is dropping."

"I know. I just used a healing pot. I don't remember the AOE radiating alongside the green stuff."

Mythic steps in, dragging the monsters away from the green. "It always has. It just does more now. Interrupt that!"

"Interrupt what? The tree's not casting."

"The satyr is."

"I got it!" Mags answers.

"Good, I am not close enough to attack. Incoming around the back side." I shift my toon and hug the walls, stepping into the small alcove that rests there. Jumping over the roots, I position her on the back side of the monster and continue to shoot, watching my arrows fly across the screen, blending with my ponies and the others in the thick of things.

More green swirls appear as I dodge them, trying to get closer to Deacon and his healing, only to hear a strangled scream through my monitor. "What the hell is that?" Next thing I know, my toon is running in fear, right across the green circles, with my health bar plummeting and unable to do anything about it. "SHIT! Deacon, I am running on death."

"I can't help Elo, I am running too."

"We all are, including Mythic!" Mags explains.

"That's not good. I don't remember this fear effect. Did we miss an interrupt or something?"

"No, it's new."

"Fan-freaking-tastic." Panning the screen, I see a black beam with blue swirls heading my toon's way. Damn, my health is already down from running over green and now it's taking another hit from a beam. I might not actually survive this. I quickly shift my toon to safety and slam both my shields up, drinking a health potion. Gold magic wraps around my character as my health jumps back up. "Thank you Deacon! I didn't even think you were within range."

"Thank the fear effect. It ran me straight to you. That's the only reason I could save yo-ass."

"Thank you, bad guys!"

Moo and Mags both laugh. "Well, we already know you love the morally grey guys!"

I chuckle at their words. "True, but mostly I love my evil red dragon, Gren."

"I read your book Elo. He's not entirely evil," Moo responds.

"Well, he was. I might have adapted him a wee bit."

"Sure, sure."

Mythic interrupts our conversation. "Hero!"

Darn it. I need to pay more attention because I didn't even notice we broke the shield off the tree. Too lost in my thoughts about Gren now as I click the button Mythic has requested, granting us all extra damage and a speed boost. Each of us now focuses on burning the boss down while the satyr casts his black magic, weaving it back around the tree to corrupt him.

I groan as I watch the tree become surrounded in black, knowing we failed in our burn. Tabbing back to the tree, I direct my ponies there and start beating on its shield once more. "Shoot. Mr. Tree is once more corrupted."

"Elo, get in close. More green circles are incoming."

"Working on it." I watch as Mythic leads the satyr away from the spawning green. Hitting my speed boost, I race my toon around the outside and am just about to reach them when that damn fear hits again.

This time, though, I didn't have the green behind me as my character ran away in fear. It's really the small things in this game. Now, Deacon can focus on healing others because Elo is not that damaged.

Once the fear effect is done, I scan the ground, noticing over three quarters of the room is full of danger. "So much green stuff. I have nowhere to stand."

"Hey, at least you are not melee. It's easier to see out there."

"True, that's why I only play tanks as melee."

"But melee is where the party is, Elo!"

"Yah, that's right. You all missed the fact that I am an introvert?"

"You are not!"

"Am too. That's why there are days I prefer to stay in the open world, where I play by myself, doing quests and rep grinding."

"Really?"

Hearing Deacon's laughter, I ask, "What?"

"Nothing, I just misheard that."

"Mishe...ard...? Oh, no you didn't!"

"Yes, I did!"

"You are bad, Deacon."

"He's not the only one, Elo."

"Damn, you are all bad. Maybe I should rage-quit and go back to writing."

"Yeh, about shrooms. Wait, I must have one in my pockets somewhere."

"You do not!"

"No, but I do have some in the kitchen."

"You just like teasing me!" I shift my toon to the side, once more avoiding the breath weapon, grateful that I am only getting every second one aimed at her and that Mythic is trying to steer it into the cave wall, away from everyone. Skirting back towards the tree, I expertly move her around the green puddles of death.

"Always Elo!"

I catch Moo's laughter at Deacon's comments, knowing I set myself up once more to be harassed. Shaking my head, I shift my screen over to the boss, returning my focus to the game. Talking for me means less damage. Less damage means the boss lasts longer, and that is bad for us. Clicking my buttons, I send another round of attacks into the boss, moving through my rotation as I keep shifting out of the green. A minute later, the boss drops and I take another swig of my Coke, grabbing a few chips before we continue further into the mists.

"What are you snacking on, Elo?"

"Chips."

"No shrooms?"

"No Deacon, no shrooms, but I WILL be buying some next time I go grocery shopping."

"I got them and they taste good, Elo. How do those chips taste?"

"Like All-Dressed normally tastes."

"I bet. You need a bit of Meursault to go with them."

"Meursault?"

"Wine, it's made in the Burgundy region of France, specifically the Côte de Beaune subregion. I went to the vineyard several times when I lived over there."

"What does it taste like?"

"Rich, buttery, and full-bodied 'cause it's primarily made from the Chardonnay grape."

"So dry then. No thanks, Mister wine connoisseur."

Deacon chuckles. "That I am, but it's not that dry. I think you will like it."

"I drink the cheap shit, Deacon, you know that. White Zin all the way. Besides, I have a pop sitting next to me right now." I summon my expensive mount, clicking the repair button to fix my gear again and sighing at the gold cost tied to it. How is a person supposed to make gold when running these things are so expensive? Spotting Mythic's toon bolting away on his pally pony, I dismount off my repair mount and call forth my pony. "I know... You all can roll your eyes, but I got standards. My mount needs to match my pets."

"I am sure you do."

"What's that supposed to mean?"

"Nothing Elo."

# Chapter Five

# Maze of Death

**M**ythic interrupts our friendly banter. "Alright, you two. Let's go, the path is clear."

Right, enough lollygagging. I watch Mags, Deacon, and Mythic ride upon their golden god horses, dressed in full plate, with heraldry hanging over its backside and tacked to their bridles. Pretty darn fancy. I can just picture it. All the pally's in the world, going to the same place to buy their horses. A stock sale since they all match perfectly.

At least Kay's toon has an elephant that he summons forth. You don't see those very often. Mine either, for that matter, a pony to match my pets - no saddle, no bridle, no fancy plate - very different from theirs. Just a white coat with a purple mane and tail, although mine does have magical fire dancing around its hooves. Oh, and a tiny little gnome perched upon its back that theirs are lacking.

Panning, I see Moo race past me on her mount, also a pony, but the midnight version. Its ebony coat glints in the light, contrasted with a dark purple mane and flames around its hooves. This group definitely has an affinity for ponies over all the other mounts out there.

Moo and I are clearly very much alike in some aspects regarding this game. It makes me wonder if she loves dragons, and if so, how much. Because while the ponies are beautiful, a red dragon holds my heart. The Red Phantom. If only I could find him in the outside world and not just in my dreams. I swear, you would never see me again.

I would retreat with Rendgren to his cave, except I gave him the love of his life in my Mystic series. Somehow, I would need to deal with her. The goddess I created. But wait, I am the author. Perhaps I can write her out of the series and put me in, instead... Or not. She would foresee that and deal with me effectively.

Reaching over, I take a drink of my Coke and glance towards the chips, finding I desire something sweeter at the moment. I don't normally crave sugar because I am a salt girl all the way, but the stress of this place is getting to me. I need sugar. Candy, cookies. Ooh, perhaps I need Oreos just like our pally tank, Ludy. He eats them every Saturday night while playing with us. I make a mental note to add sugar to my grocery list.

Urging my character across the field, I follow the others down the long pathway ahead of us. Rock walls loom on either side, with a blend of wildflowers growing at their base. A few creeping vines reach skyward but not enough to enable our characters to climb over the rock walls. Not that our characters have the climbing ability, unless they are doing a specific quest, but it's fun to think about.

At the bottom of the hill stand two centaurs, bows slung over their backs and spears in their hands. Behind them is a tiny faerie, her eyes alight with mischief as she appears to be looking right at our toons. She speaks in a chipper, cheery voice; too chipper, if you ask me. Does she not realize where we are, or that there is a clock ticking?

"Oh look, I have friends to play with."

"Moo, she's right. Do your thing and bring their friends in." Mythic happily charges his character down the hill, jumping off his pony to attack the centaurs.

With tricks of her own, the faerie laughs, its taunting tone bouncing off the stone walls surrounding us and out through my monitor. Her wings flutter and she hovers a moment before floating through the white wall behind her. "Catch me if you can!"

Since Mythic is now in combat with the centaurs, I watch the direction she flutters away, knowing we are going to need to follow her through the maze. It's like the Labyrinth all over, except there is no Goblin King waiting for us. You want to talk about romance books and the morally grey villains that readers fall in love with? Well, he's one of them. He was my first taste with that side of darkness and one I will never forget. After that, it was all downhill from there.

"The faerie went straight back in case you missed it." I click my control button and let the others know in Discord. Watching Moo's ponies bringing in friends, I guide my toon down to the acorn which is sitting to the left of where the battle is happening, knowing it's one of the resurrection points we need. Before I get her there, one centaur charges my toon, knocking her off her pony and slamming her into a wall.

Whelp, there goes half my health bar. I click my healing button quickly, seeing Deacon's magic wrap around her at the same time, which is good. It's just in time for the second one to pick up where the first did. I sigh as my toon slides down the wall again. I really need to get to that rez point because clearly the monsters are out to destroy poor Elo.

I mutter beneath my breath to the others in the group. "Damn centaurs, why don't they love gnomes as much as I do?"

"You're the only one who does Elo!"

"Na-ah. I see them all the time in town!" Sending my toon's ponies in, I run my character over and click on the cog-wheel, ignoring the scrawling script. I just click yes, activate. Good, at least if I die from those damn mobs, I can come back here and not the beginning of this place. "Restore point activated. We are ready."

"Good, let's kill these and hunt ourselves a faerie."

"I like faeries. Why can't we just be her friend?"

"Elo, that's not how this works!"

"I know, but the hope is there. Did you know that you can leave a saucer of milk out for them to be friendly?"

"Do you have one of those in your inventory?"

"No, I don't think it exists in the game actually, now that I think about it."

"With the amount of cats running around, it should."

"You're right. I will need to look into that. Perhaps make a suggestion." Watching the ponies on my screen pound away at the monsters, I click my attacks, working through my rotation and watching my numbers rise on the damage meters. Seeing the centaur turn, knowing it's coming for my character, I race her around to stand next to Deacon, intending to use him as a shield. Only it doesn't matter, the creature gets to my toon first, sending her flying backwards. "Why me? There are four others in this dungeon to charge! I don't see you attacking them, you stupid monsters."

"That's because you are the only ranged Elo. They like ranged. It's possible that if you get closer, they might mistake you for melee," Mythic chuckles.

"I don't think that's going to work," I answer. "Besides, I can't see anything up close. Ranged is better."

"You're probably right, but at least in melee we can cleave." As the centaur runs back, we do enough damage to defeat him, along with the others.

"I have AoE! That's like cleave!"

Mythic bolts through the wall after the faerie before the body has even stopped moving.

"No tricking you." The faerie's voice once more echoes all around our characters, followed by the tinkling of bells mixed with laughter. The lanterns hanging in the doorways flash, brightening the darkness of the maze. One that we, as a group, have nicknamed the maze of death.

I follow Mythic with my character, not even bothering to call a mount, watching the wall dissolve behind me as I step into the next room. The others are already knee-deep in battle with a variety of creatures, but someone's got to solve the puzzle. And, of course, that someone is me.

I circle along the outer edges, examining the runes carved into the hollow stumps of trees, each stump positioned at an exit from the square room we're trapped in. Another box surrounded by walls. I'll admit, I'm a little disappointed that no one thought to toss a minotaur in here, just patrolling around at random. Wouldn't that be a riot? We're already fighting mobs, and then bam, bonus beast crashing the party.

Committing the rune to memory, I pan the screen and immediately spot chargers in the pack. Great. I sprint my character to the next rune and drop a trap at her feet, praying it'll slow them down long enough for me to do my job. My ponies charge into the fray, followed by a rapid-fire barrage of arrows. Just because I'm on puzzle duty doesn't mean I get to slack on damage.

I click the second tree, only to watch my character go flying. Seriously? He ran right over the trap and ignored it? Damn, I really hate these centaurs.

Righting my character, I drop another trap, spreading a sticky mess between her and the incoming enemies as I move her toward the third rune. The moment I examine it, I notice the differences between the three. This rune isn't like the other two. That's promising.

Skirting the edge of the fight, I head for the final stump, just as something shifts at the edge of the screen. Catching the movement, I quickly jump my toon back, barely dodging a charging mob. "Hah! Not catching me that time!"

Finishing the pathing, I click on the last rune, mentally cycling through them until I pinpoint the odd one out. With a quick tap, I drop a purple marker on the ground near it for the others to follow. Then I shift my full attention back to the fight, knowing they'll need my damage. Though, judging by how smoothly they're handling things, maybe not. It doesn't take long to clear the pack, and just like that, we're back on Mythic's heels, chasing him through the path I marked.

I step my toon into yet another room, just like the last one. Repetitive much? Then again, it *is* a maze. Consistency is kind of the point. These rooms aren't meant to be unique; they're meant to trap the unlucky souls banished here forever.

Stone walls rise around us, three more exits blocked off. Great. Another round of *find the right door.*

With a sigh, I pan my screen toward the center of the room, just in time to see swirling lights coalesce into a massive dragon. Purple scales gleam in the low light of the maze, and its glowing green eyes lock onto Mythic. Perfect. Let him be the chew toy this time. Wait... is that saliva dripping from its fangs? No way. That had to be a glitch. Right? "Did you guys see that?"

"See what?"

"The saliva dripping from its mouth."

"Are you sure it's not your own, Elo? It is a dragon, after all," Mags teases.

"Yes, I am sure. Besides, as much as purple is my favorite color, the dragon needs to be red for me to drool. And that one is clearly drool-worthy."

"I think you drool over all dragons. The silver one in Maddie's is pretty darn fine," Moo replies.

"True! I do love Lucy. He was a fun character to create. So was Maddie, actually. She's my neighbor's book girlfriend."

"Lucy? He?" Deacon asks. "Isn't that a woman's name?"

"Shoot! Sorry! Spoiler there. Maddie nicknamed Lucian, Lucy in my story."

"Why would she do that?"

Moo laughs. "You gotta read the books, Deacon."

"That's right, I already gave you a spoiler. No more."

"I am not much of a reader, Elo. You gotta tell me."

"Give me my shrooms and I might!"

"No way, those shrooms are mine."

Laughing, I move my character around the room, loving the group dynamic. People that don't play MMOs, don't understand the family that builds through this game. The connections we all enjoy, even if we are just hanging around on the Discord server chatting. Though right now, we should be focusing. I can just imagine what others would think of our casual, not casual run. "Did you all notice that dragon's claws are the same size as my toon?"

"That's because you are a gnome Elo... Small and puntable!"

"Aren't Rendgren's claws the same size as a truck?" Moo asks.

"That's different!"

"How so?"

"It's Rendgren! Rendgren is a boss! This dragon doesn't even have a name! Nothing but an oversized trash mob, essentially."

"The Mystic is a boss Elo and you are just mad that it's not red."

"You're probably right. If only the game had one! I would tame it immediately." Shifting my character around while tapping my attack buttons, I move her over to the next rune, clicking on it just as the dragon spins to face her. Realizing that a breath weapon is coming my toon's way, I jump her back and click my speed boost, hearing my addon screaming at me as it clips her backside. "Damn, things hurt in here."

"It's a nine Elo. Gotta stay out of the breath."

"I was trying. I wasn't expecting it to spin that quickly. It was aimed at Deacon!"

"That's because he realized I wasn't a gnome and I gave it gold!"

"That is *soo* not the case! Gnomes are cute, and you can't pay the bad guys."

"Why not? They do it on TV shows all the time."

"Yes, cause that's TV. This is a game! It's different."

I work my way around the room to the markers, dropping a flag at the gate we need to pass through. With that done, I turn to face the dragon; just in time to see a glowing pool spawn beneath it and hear my monitor yell at me to move it. Great. My tanking and damage addons are overlapping. I watch its health spike before Mythic moves it and I mutter a soft curse. "Damn dragon, healing itself while damaging us? Why don't we get magic like that?"

"We do. The priest has it. They send a purple wave out that heals us and damages monsters. Druids have one as well, sparkle beams that aggro mobs while healing us. But when both of them do that, it pulls everything, and I mean *everything*. Even things from other rooms or floors."

"Right, so where is this so-called priest or druid, then?"

"We have Deacon!"

"Yes, but he's a pally... Deacon! Where's your circle of death to them and life to us?"

"I don't need one!"

"Are you sure about that?"

"Yes, I have pally prisms!" An aura of sparkling lights surrounds his character, expanding into rainbows that dance off his armor and ricochet into the group and the monster.

"Right. Just what you need. Something that makes you look angelic!"

"It's a lifestyle yo... you either pally mindset or you ain't."

"Clearly I ain't!" Dodging another breath weapon, I send a volley of arrows into it as Mythic, Mags, and Moo drag the dragon down and snuff out his life. Walking my character over to the body, I kneel her down and type emotes in chat.

"What are you doing Elo?" Deacon asks.

"Taking a scale of course!"

"You can't do that in game!"

"Why not? Read the chat. It says it right there. *Elotarra kneels and carves a scale off the dragon, tucking it in her backpack.* They are purple and I might as well pretend my character is here."

"You are crazy!"

"That's right! Even my nephews and nieces call me Crazy Auntie Randi! I got a reputation to uphold."

"Not going there."

Laughing, I turn my toon and follow the others through the gate. "I might be crazy, but you all dragged me in here, so you are just as crazy!"

"No comment."

As I step my character into the room, I wonder how many rooms we will have this run. Sometimes it seems short, other times it seems like we take the long route, but I am sure it's all equal. It's just the perception that it's not. Seeing the mobs fill the room quickly, I tab through them, knowing somewhere in this pack there are healers and I want to focus on one. They usually are there in the room after the solo fight. I hit my cap-locks and mark one. "I got white!"

"I will get the other with my shield, though I can probably get both."

"Of course you can. Pally is the favored child of this game." Muttering softly, I shift my character out of a pool on the ground and head towards the runes.

When Ludy and I used to challenge each other, he used the shield often, slamming into the side of my bear's head, causing damage to her health. Pretty certain if the game had it, there would be little yellow birds fluttering around my character's head like they do in the cartoons. Each of them chirping loud enough to cause more damage. Not that the bash helped him. My bear is tough.

We dueled for thirty-nine minutes in town, with spectators gathering and cheering us on. They were probably taking bets between themselves. Who would win? The favored child, or the guardian. I ended up winning because he foolishly ran next to a cliff and I cast a wind spell to knock him. Over he went, plummeting to his death, or near death. Enough so that I won the match because he *fled the battlefield*. It was all good fun.

Afterwards, he had to go to bed because he hadn't expected the duel to go so long. Neither had I, actually. I was pretty proud of that accomplishment. Normally I get trounced. Two second trounced, depending on who challenges me. Yes, my thoughts immediately drift to Chains, who loves to duel, because he's usually the one destroying me after I dare to click accept.

Reaching the second tree stump, I spot the purple flag sitting at the doorway, already marking the path. "Who did that?"

"I did," Mythic replies.

"First you all steal my shroom and now you steal my job!"

Mythic chuckles. "I know the path now, Elo. Pew-pew. Kill them all."

"How?"

"Add-on."

"And it works? I had one back when this was current, but it never worked properly."

"It does."

"Well, that makes things easy."

Deacon laughs with him. "You should write a book about this too, Elo! First, we steal your shrooms, and now your rune job. I wonder what else we can steal."

Seriously, if I could stomp on his feet, I would have my gnome do that. Oh wait, I can emote it. "I might just have to do that. And write about all the mean things you are doing. Picking on my poor little gnome."

"That's what gnomes are for!"

"Gnomes are cute and adorable! I at least have Moo and Mags on my side."

"Are you sure about that?"

"Yes, I am..." Hmmm, silence is never a good thing. I can picture them averting their gaze from me and it draws a sigh from my lips.

Mags is the first to speak up. "Sorry Elo. It's all about the space goats. There is no comparison, especially when they dance."

"Hey, gnomes can dance!"

"Not like goats can."

"True. You do have all the smexy moves. In my opinion, they are the best in the game, though the elves are a close second. My gnome just hops around like she's completely clueless in the art of dance."

I think back to my old hunter, Milosh. The one I played back when Mags was my GM. I had a goat, too. And the way they twirled their hips with all the right moves. Sure, we call them space goats, but I swear it's tied to their sylvan or satyr heritage. Myths and legends are full of tales about them luring mortals to their doom with song and dance.

Deep in the woods, or up on an inn table, shaking their booty for gold. And boy, did they rake it in. I tried it with both Elo and Milosh and Milosh tripled Elo's income. Poor little gnomie. Even her ponies dance with more grace, rearing back on their hind legs and pummeling enemies with their front hooves as they charge through the battlefield. "But what about my fantastic purple hair and those big, adorable violet eyes?"

Moo chuckles. "You are adorable Elo. Don't listen to them."

"Thanks Moo." Seeing the healer casting, I click my stun button, aiming to stop her cast, only to see the message flash across my screen that Mythic had interrupted it, likely with his shield bashing into the monster's head. "Right, so now Mythic is stealing my stuns."

"You just gotta pick the ones I am not targeting, Elo."

"You target them ALL Mythic!"

"It might seem that way, but I don't. Just watch where my focus is."

"Right, I can do that, or I can just mark the one I am on and you leave it alone!"

"Sure, if you guarantee to get all the interrupts!"

"As a hunter?" I laugh into the Discord at their teasing. "No way, I am a clicker, remember? I actually have to move my mouse to cast my spells and use it to move my toon. If I am dodging stuff, you are all out of luck."

Seeing the centaur pivot on the screen and face where my toon is standing, I groan, knowing I am getting charged again. Clicking my defensives, I watch my toon flung back and slide down the wall. "I really wish the characters could actually stomp their feet and glare at the enemies."

"Yo Elo, it won't work. Nothing is scared of gnomes!" Deacon laughs at the thought. "But it would be amusing to see it. So threatening you are! I can feel my knees shaking. Here, have some healing for those wounds."

"Deacon!" Having succeeded in its charge, I watch the centaur turn and run back to Mythic. "I saw it coming and protected myself this time. He barely hurt me." Only to groan in dismay as I watch the second one charge my toon and slam her back, earning more laughter from those in Discord.

"No, he just sent his friend after you. Tag team the gnome. I love it!" Deacon replies.

"Hey! That's so not fair." I scan through my buttons, noticing the one I want is greyed out. "Damn, my heals are down."

"I got you Elo!" Deacon chants a few words, channeling his healing magic around my toon. "That's why I am here."

"Yes, but you're supposed to be focusing on Mythic. I need to avoid things better."

"Bah, I got you all! I am the healer, after all."

I shift my toon across the room, positioning her behind Deacon, knowing a walking plate shield would be even better. This way, if they charged her, they would hit him first. I should have been here the entire run. Turning my attention back to the mobs, I send in an array of attacks, watching as, one by one, the mobs in the group drop to our attacks.

Panning the screen around, automatically looking for sparkles, I see Mythic race through the gate where the blue flag sits, hearing the faerie's voice congratulating us for choosing correctly. Glancing over at the clock ticking on the upper right-hand side of my screen, I notice we are about halfway done. Damn, we need to pick up speed.

I race after them with Deacon at my side, entering the next room, just like all the others. The only difference is, instead of a group of mobs, there is a giant frog. Just like the dragon, it towers over top of all the players' toons, especially my gnome. I shake my head, knowing that normally, you only get one mini boss in the maze, and yet, we got two. When did this change?

I shift over as Mythic, Moo and Mags step in to engage it, staying just at range of my attacks. I watch it turn, lashing its tongue out in my character's direction, jumping my character back so that she's not hit. As she lands, a green pool of sludge spawns beneath her feet and I adjust her over to be closer to Deacon. "What the hell? Why me?"

"Cause you are a tiny little fly to it," Moo replies as she skirts around the frog, rushing into battle with Mythic.

Deacon chuckles. "Tasty gnome."

Mags follows, her laughter filling the Discord. "Poor Elo, the monsters are out to get her."

Glancing at the screen, realizing that no matter where I position my toon in the room, the frog is going to get her. I mutter under my breath. "How does a tongue reach that far?"

"You do know how frogs actually catch flies, right Elo...?"

"Yes, Deacon, I know. I just never paid attention to the actual reach compared to their body size." I shift my character out of its reach again and launch a few more arrows into it while I click my ponies' rage, wanting to defeat this thing as fast as we can.

"Being such a small gnome, I think that would be something you should pay attention to. There are creatures all over the world that eat things your size."

"Yes, well, I guess I have been lucky then."

"Or you haven't fought any real monsters."

"Hey! I'm in here with you and nothing has eaten me yet!"

Deacon chuckles. "Only time will tell."

Mythic shifts the frog out of the green pool. "More pew-pew!"

"Too busy dodging the tongue, Mythic." Seeing the green shimmer appear beneath her feet again, I shift my character. "And those wretched green pools of death. How is one supposed to manage damage in here?"

"Better positioning?"

"Yah-yah." I jump my character back as the frog launches her way, knowing if it actually landed on her, she would be toast. No amount of healing would save her. "Stoopid frog. You know, small is not always good." Shifting my toon over to the back side where Mags and Moo are fighting, I send another round of attacks against it. Watching it spin my character's way, again, I curse and shift her out of the way, only to watch it collapse beneath our attacks. Mythic chuckles. "No more frogs, Elo. Only big bugs and a faerie."

"I know, and they don't eat gnomes."

"Who knows what's changed in here, Elo? They might this time around."

"That's true. Everything beyond the mists is always changing."

Mythic turns his character and leads them through the last gate, stopping at the edge of the clearing as he waits momentarily for the rest of us.

# Chapter Six

# Faerie's Revenge

"Ya'ay! You found me. Now we can play a game!"

I follow Mythic through the gate, getting annoyed at the faerie taunting us every time we pass through a door, despite knowing it is part of the game. But really, it just implies that we are not clever enough for her tricks. That being said, there have been times we have chosen the wrong path, destined to be sent back to the beginning. Panning the area, I take in the scene. The faerie we have been chasing, hovering before us on a small island. If you could call it an island.

Water flows from the mountains to the right, skirting along the outer edge between us and the faerie before tumbling over the cliff's edge, disappearing into the depths below. Moss and flowers grow in a spiral pattern, radiating outward. Honestly, it would be a peaceful, picturesque scene... if not for the rotten little fae in the middle, leaving a trail of monsters in her wake and laughing at our struggles.

A few cranes wade through the stream, their beaks dipping into the water as they hunt for fish and bugs hidden beneath the surface.

On our side of the stream, I spot the second mushroom field and guide Elo toward it, only to watch three pally's zoom past, dismount, and start scarfing down mushrooms like it's a buffet. Seriously?

I weave Elo between them and spot one near another gate, this one leading back into the maze. I grab it and mutter into Discord, "Sure, steal my shrooms again!"

"Every time Elo! I am stuffing extra in my bags this time!"

"You can't do that. The game doesn't allow it."

"Sure can! I am an expert at breaking rules."

"In real life, perhaps!"

Mythic chuckles. "Alright. I hope everyone is ready, 'cause I am charging in now."

"Yep, ready." It's always a good sign when the tank checks in before pulling the boss, though in this room, it's pretty open, so there's no actual risk of getting locked out. And yes, that can happen. I remember one where we were facing off against the Norse gods. One of my friends, Vyn, challenged me to a damage race. I accepted, naturally. The tank pulled the boss. We both blew all our cooldowns... and then I heard him swearing. I panned my camera back just in time to see the gates slam shut, locking him outside the boss room. All his cooldowns? Wasted. Guess he failed his reflex save to get knocked inside with the rest of us. We still tease him about it to this day.

I think that was the same one where my friend Magic lost his trust in me. I told him it was a level two and he brought his baby priest. And really, in my defense, I honestly thought it was a two. The first set of mobs he was muttering at how difficult it was to heal, and how he might go back to his main. When we looked at the number below the clock, it was a twelve. Ooops. He has never forgiven me for that one and double checks now, every time we ask him to play.

Our characters splash through the water towards the faerie. This game really does have some amazing visuals. I stand Elo back and wait, having learned in the past that attacking before the tank usually means the death of my character. Seeing Mythic's hammer bounce off the faerie, I send my ponies in and let loose with the first round of my attacks, just as Mags and Moo charge in beside Mythic.

"I have a game. Let's play!"

"Is it wrong that I don't want to play with the faerie?" I mutter under my breath behind the scenes. That I want to go back to the outside world and putter. Or better yet, run to my kitchen and grab another Coke because mine is becoming dangerously low. Perhaps some popcorn. But I can't because there is a timer, counting down the seconds. Don't get me wrong. I love playing with the others, but I have done this one, again and again, back in the day and I am over it.

I spot the silver orbs of light circling the faerie, materializing into balls large enough to flatten any player unlucky enough to get hit. I sidestep with my toon just in time, watching one barrel past me. The others follow suit, dodging like pros. No squished players. That will make Deacon happy.

"Let's have a tea party with friends!"

The faerie's words sound through my monitor, causing me to shift in my chair. That's right, this one is all about the games. I guess I tuned it out. It's easy to do when there are new ones filling my brain. To the left on my screen, magic shimmers and coalesces, joining into something solid, like a cross between several creatures. Pointed face like a fox, long ears like a rabbit, with the silver fur and the bushy tail of a squirrel. Its body is short to the ground and lean, like a weasel, meant for hunting. Coal-black eyes spark with blue light as they focus solely on Mags.

Knowing I have no ability to dispel that magic, I drop one of my many traps at its feet, hoping to keep it contained long enough that the magic would wear out, because I recall it's only here for about ten seconds. That being said, those ten seconds are the longest ones ever, when it's chasing your toon around.

Seeing it immobilized, I grin to myself. Brownie points to the hunter. Wait, did it just break my trap? Dammit! "What the? It broke my trap and is running again! Watch yourselves." I tab over to it, hoping I can kill it before it reaches Mags, because we really need her damage on the faerie.

Mythic pulls the faerie away so that Mags can continue to fight, and not get struck by whatever was summoned. Moments later, it fades back into the nether where it was called from.

"Well, that one didn't work. Let's play another game. Find me if you can!"

I can just picture the faerie clapping her hands again in delight, just from the chipper tone of her voice. Illusions of her appear around the perimeter of the rock, looking very much like what she did with subtle differences. I quickly pan over them, committing them to memory as I pick out the differences. "There, the one by the cliff edge. She's the one that doesn't belong." Turning my toon her way, I click on the illusion and send Bounce and Downy in to attack, watching them race across the screen and pound on it with their hooves.

Lights dance in the middle of the room as another creature spawns right beside me. I watch it turn its body, realizing rather suddenly that I am its focus this time. "Damn, this one's chasing me!"

"You should be able to outrun it, Elo. It has shorter legs than you, and that's a hard thing to do," Deacon says.

"Fun...ney, Deacon." Damn, I hate having to run and use spells that require me to click them. It makes life so much harder. I shift my mouse over and drop a trap in front of me, running my character over it and positioning her just out of reach on the other side, watching it succumb to my effect. "Right, make sure no one targets it!" Turning my attacks back to the illusion, I watch the others fade away as the real faerie appears once more.

"Clever creatures, you found me! Let's play ball again."

Seeing the balls forming again, I shift over, only to see that I have stepped into Mags' path. Damn, I hate being close. I keep going, breathing a sigh of relief as the ball rolls out past my toon, knowing that if it wasn't just a video game character, she would feel it grazing her backside. That was too close for comfort. I shift my toon back to range. This is exactly why I don't play melee unless I am a tank that can take hits like that.

Watching Mythic taunt the faerie back to the middle, I take a quick glance over to the faerie's health bar in the upper left corner of my screen. Great. Three quarters of it left. That means another few rounds of all her delightful games.

Hearing her chatter again about bringing in friends, I pan around, seeing it spawning on the left side of the group. Shifting my character over, I click my trap and position it on the coalescing lights. Smiling as icicles wrap around it instantly. Now let's hope it stays there. Nope, I watch as it runs into the group, trapping Mags and Moo in bubbles, rolling around at the boss's feet.

I giggle, reminding myself of the videos I see while soaking in my tub. Large clear plastic balls that people get into and roll down hills, or into each other. They actually look like a lot of fun. It makes me want to go push them around in the game, but I know that it's not an option.

Deacon chuckles. "I got you two… dispel incoming."

"Aww Deacon, I wanted to roll them around the battlefield, like they do in those videos."

"It's too bad the game doesn't allow it."

"Yes, it is."

Once Deacon dispels them, we return to fighting, only to see illusions pop up around us again. I look them over, trying to figure out the difference, but this time, Mythic is faster than me. He charges across the room to the one I am standing near and starts attacking it. Turning my toon around, I click on it and start my assault on it, only to have to run again from the creature appearing next to me. I skirt around the outside, keeping out of its range, all the while clicking my attacks.

It isn't long, with another few rounds of dodging the balls, playing with the creature and picking the difference out, that we finally defeat the faerie. Well, we don't really kill her, she's just done playing with us. Apparently, she does think she's our friend, and this is her way of showing it. Yes, that's right. Friends. I love friends that try to kill me with their games. They are the bestest!

Deacon looks over our health bars and heals most of us up to full. The only one he doesn't is Mythic. That is because he has already charged across the room and launched himself over the waterfall.

"Let's Gooooo! Tick-Tock!"

# Chapter Seven

# Pathway of Bugs

I race my toon forward and try to peer over the edge of the cliff that Mythic just jumped from, waiting for one of three things - the splat of his body along with his health bar plummeting to zero, the groan of pain if he survived striking the ground, or the splash of water meaning he jumped correctly. Not that I would actually hear that, but it was fun to think of.

I am very much aware that if you didn't jump just right, it's a fall to your character's death. Something I have done several times in the past. Placement is everything, and it has been a while since she was in here last. Several years actually, and while Mythic clearly didn't care with the way he launched himself, my toon doesn't have the same stamina and health that he does, what with being a hunter compared to his tanky constitution. The risk is there.

"Jump Elo! The water is fine."

"No sharks down there?"

"Nope, just crocodiles!"

"Right, just crocs. Mythical beings that are apparently everywhere in Florida, yet when I went down there to meet Ludy, I saw none, and I was looking."

"That's because they were all hiding from you, Elo," Deacon snickers.

"They were not!" I jump my character off the cliff, watching her descend against the backdrop of the waterfall.

"Wee, squish the gnome!"

Hearing Deacon, I pan my screen up, seeing him falling just above her. Great, my toon is about to get landed on by a pally in full plate. If this were real life, there is no way she would survive that, even if they are landing in water. Wait, I wonder if I have gliders in my bag to get out of this.

Opening the side panel, I quickly scan my inventory, recalling just as my toon strikes the water, they are in my bank back in town. Great place for them to be. What was I thinking? I swim my character towards the land, grateful there is no drag from Deacon's landing. Otherwise, I would likely need to have my character kick off his plate chest just to avoid drowning. "Nice Deacon! You could have waited instead of deliberately landing on my toon!"

"Like Mythic said Elo, clocks-a-ticking! Gotta go!"

Behind them, the splashes of Mags and Moo follow, each one clambering out of the lake to shake off. "We still have time. It's only the bugs left." I shift my character over to the acorn, clicking on the cog-wheel to activate the rez point. Would do no good to rez all the way at the beginning of the maze. It's a long run back. Seeing Moo and Mags race past, I turn my toon to follow, looking over the landscape ahead of them.

Narrow dirt paths wind and twist between gnarled tree roots and jagged rock spires. Oversized wood-bugs skitter along, some wider than the ledges they're crawling on. Normally, these things fit in the palm of your hand, no bigger than a curled-up pea, but these? These are the size of horses, with the bulk of small elephants. Giant mosquitoes buzz overhead in slow, predatory circles, definitely on the hunt.

So much dirt... The only saving grace is that this is a video game. Which means my cute white fur onesie won't end up stained or smelling like a wet dog; despite the virtual dunking it took earlier. Something I am all too familiar with since I am a dog groomer three days of the week.

The first thing I do when I get home? Soak in a vanilla-scented bath. Technically, it's *Birthday Cake* from Island Soap on Salt Spring, though their *Unicorn Sparkle*, which smells like a blend of cotton candy and vanilla is a close second. True vanilla though, that's always been my jam... Even my perfume is vanilla.

Back in high school, my friends used to joke that Betty Crocker exploded in my locker. Sadly, The Body Shop stopped making their oils, so I'm now on the eternal quest for the perfect vanilla replacement and buying it online through second-hand sellers is out of my price range.

Pivoting my character back to the battle, I send my ponies into attack and watch them kick up dirt as they charge towards the bugs. Yep, again I state, it's a good thing our outfits do not get dirty in this game.

I watch the bugs turn towards my toon, spitting slops of green towards Deacon and I. Shifting her to the left, I click a few of my attacks, skirting out even further as more acid strikes the surrounding ground.

Deacon's curse draws a chuckle from my lips, knowing he didn't move fast enough to avoid the acid. Glancing at his health bar verifies it. "That's what you get for wearing plate armor. Slow and cumbersome. Mail allows you to move better."

Mags teases both of us. "Cloth is even better, but we don't have any in this group."

"I could get my mage, but he's too squishy and not up to par yet to enter the mists," Deacon comments.

"True, Mine is too. She's been hanging around town hunting spell books."

Mythic mutters into the Discord, guiding his character along the pathway. "More pew-pew, less talky-talky."

"But Mythic! Social! Isn't that why you invited me?"

"But Elo, timer! Social after."

"Right." I watch Deacon's toon run forward and down the narrow ledge that the bugs like to cluster on, following cautiously with mine. It makes me wonder about the coding that allows the bugs to stay on it, even with knock back effects, whereas a wrong move with our mouse or keys, and our toon is plummeting to their death.

At least my character is tiny. I have more room to navigate. All I need to do is keep her smack dab in the middle of the path and she's safe. Especially knowing the bugs can stomp with enough power to shake the ground and knock them off. Been there, done that, when it was active back in the day; don't want to do it again. The fall alone was bad enough, let alone having your soul ripped from your body upon impact.

Then your soul gets to return to the nearest graveyard, where you make a choice. Face the judgement of the priestess or run back to your body and hope you can find it, and that no one has looted it. We loot monsters, so why can't they loot us? It never happens, though. Our body is always there, loot and all, which is good. No one would venture out of town if that was the case. Sometimes, though, you need to accept the priestess's help, because you can't get back to your body, but it comes at a cost.

I can just imagine, standing before the priestess, hoping that she's busy with some other soul, so that you can slip around and click the return to life button like in the TV show *Drop Dead Diva*. Or needing to explain why your toon died and hope they believe your sorry excuse, whatever it might be, that day. And I will admit, some of them are pretty darn sorry.

Leaving my character in a lake, and going to get food, forgetting that she actually needs to breathe in the game, thus drowning. Falling out of one of the elfin trees because I missed the bend and plummeted to my death. Really, who makes ramps that thin? Darn nimble elves. I am so not willing to admit that my hunter has an ability to save herself from those falls that I never use. Granted, this cliff meant death. There was no saving your character.

Then there is thinking that you are in a safe zone, and tabbing out of the game, or looking at the map, missing the fact that a monster is ripping her apart. Or flying into no-man's-land and unable to get back to her body. Did that a few times when I put her on auto-fly and went to get a snack.

I can picture Elo shuffling her feet at the priestess, leveling a look down at her and arching a brow. One that questions whether she was paying attention to the drain on her soul as she was flying away from the mainland. Of course she wasn't. If she was, she wouldn't be here, right?

Now, not all were my fault. Sometimes the game hates your character. There is the cranky sleeping otter that one-shotted my tank with no warning. Kay didn't even have time to heal me before I was dead. I recall him asking what happened. I wasn't even sure until I looked at the logs. Solilque at full health, healing needed, zero. Otter attack. Insta-death. Not something that should happen to a tank in the wilds. We have protections against that. Damn, they mean business.

Another time, Kay and I were off exploring. We'd pulled out a map, studied it like seasoned cartographers, and confidently concluded that we could fly from one continent to another. The distance didn't look that bad. Other islands were spaced about the same. No big deal. Totally doable.

The game sun was setting, casting golden-orange light across the calm ocean. A soft breeze stirred ripples on the water, everything was peaceful and perfect. We were halfway across, soaring free, feeling smug about our brilliant plan, when the sky crackled. A bolt of lightning arced down out of nowhere, smiting my character and mount, in one glorious, electrified instant. No warning, no nothing. Dead. Just... gone.

I know the *'powers that be'* zapped my ass back to land, with a direct warning that we had gone out of bounds.

Next thing I know, she is staring up at the priestess, pleading her case. Of course, her excuse did not entail wanting to help her friends, or that they needed her damage, or it wasn't her fault she died, which it wasn't. It was mine at pushing the boundaries of the game and my toon is suffering for it. And for that matter, Kay's toon should be standing right here with her, but he wasn't. Somehow, he escaped the wrath of the powers of creation.

No, this time, I had to admit we were exploring territory we should not have been. I tried to get back to my body, but it was well above my head, suspended in mid-air. I even took a screen-shot because no one would believe me. So I ended up returning to the priestess and accepting her help. Now, when I mentioned side effects, I was not lying. Most deaths cost about twenty to eighty gold for me because I am good at avoiding things. This one was over eleven hundred gold in repairs.

Now, the best scenario is when your healer friends call you back to your body. No running, no pleading, just return to the fray as if you never left it. Especially the druids, because some of them restore your food buff when they bring you back. I love when that happens, because then you don't need to try to eat between fights to get your buff back.

Hearing my monitor screaming at me, I pull from my thoughts about all the reasons for my toons' deaths. I see green all over and click on my shields, following the others down the ramp. Seeing the cast bar of the bug, I know that his knock back effect is incoming and I brace my toon in the middle. I see my ponies thrown across the screen, but being a game, they race back into the fray as if it never happened.

Mythic hits the bottom of the hill, pausing at the fork in the path. "Wait here." He charges to the right and throws his hammer, bouncing it off the mob's heads. We hear him chuckle in Discord as his character returns to the fork, passes us and charges into the next group.

Oh, so we are pulling two packs. That means all my abilities! I love it when things like this align and my damage on the meters skyrockets. We all wait, our fingers twitching on our keyboards as they lumber past our characters, knowing to attack them before Mythic has them secure means they turn on us and kill us.

"Alright, let loose!" Mythic says.

I tab through, finding the one with the highest health and mark it. Afterwards, I move through my rotation, sending my pets in along with extras that I have called, bouncing through my buttons in the correct order, or at least I hope I am. Effects sparkle on the screen, from the pally's golden auras, to my arrows zipping into the mobs. Doing my best to dodge the green sludge that the monsters are dropping beneath my toon's feet, while cursing the narrow platforms and having to move more than I desire. And yet, the bugs just trundle along as if it's nothing.

Movement on my screen draws my attention to the mosquitoes flying our way. Panning to the mobs, I look over all their health bars, suspecting by their route they are joining the battle shortly. There is no way we are killing the group fast enough.

Again, these things are oversized for what they should be. Can you imagine the bite from one of them? The small pesky ones are bad enough, let alone one twice the size of her character. Imagine if they bite you. It would be worse than a vampire. These would drain you dry in seconds, whereas if a vamp did that, at least you would have an afterlife as one. Much better options there.

Speaking of which, memories filter in my mind of them jumping out to the range to attack, with a chance to knock us back. Clicking my trap button, I drop it between the mobs and my toon. A little trick I learned a long time ago to stop charging mobs and most of the time, it seemed to work. The centaurs in this place, on the other hand, clearly ignored them. "Hah, now let's see if you get me, bugs."

Mythic chuckles. "They are not going to get you, Elo. I have them all."

"I am talking about the pat coming in, Mythic."

"Where?"

"To your right. Flying blood suckers."

"I got them!"

I shift my character, positioning her to safety as the stomp comes in once more, not wanting to have flying lessons at the moment. Someone else does, though. I hear Deacon's curse and catch the glint of gold off to the side of my screen. Panning over, I watch him fly through the air and over the edge. "Damn Deacon. You missed the stomp."

"You don't know that!"

"Really? I saw it on my screen. Too bad I wasn't streaming. I would watch it over and over." Moving my toon over, the toes of her yeti outfit hanging over the edge, I pan down and peer into the space below, certain that if he could, his character would be flapping his arms, trying to slow his fall. "And I am currently watching you fall!"

"Do you see your shrooms in my hand?"

"Nooo! Deacon!!! Those are my shrooms!"

"Yo, they are mine foreverrrr!!"

"Why!"

"Because I can Elo!"

"You wish, Deacon. The game doesn't allow you to keep my shrooms!"

"Today it does!"

Laughing, I watch his health bar grey out, imagining the poof of dirt rising from the ground below at his character's impact. Just like Road Runner. No, wait, it was Coyote that often had the poof of dirt. The Road Runner always outsmarted him.

Hearing the warning that the ground is going to shake, I mutter under her breath, thinking if I didn't pay attention, it would be my toon down there and Deacon would have bragging rights too. I might even have a chance to reclaim my imaginary shroom if I was fast enough.

That being said, death was instant down there, and coming back to life rarely included food, which is what that mushroom is. Though some players in my guild took the time to learn the recipes that granted them the ability to make feasts where the food persisted through death... Alas, none of them here did.

Positioning my toon back in the middle, I shift her to help Mythic, Moo, and Mags, waiting for them to curse me for watching Deacon's fall to death. Though secretly, they were probably watching and laughing inside too, at the fact that he would fail a mechanic like that. They just won't admit it. Besides, it's not like my ponies weren't still attacking, or my arrows were still striking. I just took a break in my rotation.

When no one comments, I breathe an inward sigh of relief. Clearly, they were too involved with the bugs to notice. Phew. Turning my attention to the fight, I watch as a bug jumps to my toon, getting stuck in the trap that was still there. My toon takes aim at point blank, knowing it makes no difference, but it makes me, as the player, feel better. Especially with its health bar so low. Seeing it run back to Mythic, I curse softly into Discord. "Bah, stupid bug. That was supposed to kill you."

Deacon chuckles as his toon stops beside mine. "You think a pointy stick is going to get past that armor? Wood-bugs have tough plating!"

"Welcome back. Did you enjoy your death?"

"Of course. I stopped to have a Meursault with the priestess and together we finished off the mushrooms."

"Bullshit! You lost the shroom, and it's probably still sitting there in all the dirt at the bottom."

"You will never know Elo. Just know it was tast'teee."

"Did you at least have a decent excuse?" I can feel the smile on my lips as I shift in my chair, suddenly realizing that the cartoon I watched as a kid must have been just like this. Where the Coyote had a rez point too, cause he always came back to life, no matter what happened to him. It makes me wonder what excuses he gave to the priestess that waited. He was wily enough, he probably had some good ones. Even I could think of a few that would work perfectly. "Hey Deacon, I have some excuses for you for falling."

"I don't want to hear them."

Mags snickers. "I do! Let's hear them, Elo!"

"Right, first excuse is: *I didn't die, I just briefly visited a lower elevation. Rapidly. At terminal velocity...* And the second one is: *I didn't fall, the ground betrayed me.*"

"How did you come up with those?"

"I was thinking of the Coyote chasing the Road Runner and what his excuses would be, cause Deacon reminded me of him when he hit the ground and the little poof of dirt rose from it."

"You and that mental mind Elo," Mythic replies.

"Hey, I am an author! I freely admit my mind is mental." I can see Mythic rolling his eyes in my mind from the tone laced in his comment.

"At least she admits she's crazy."

Laughing and rolling my own eyes, I take a sip of my Coke. "Yes. Crazy enough to be dragged into here, when I could be writing all these fantastic ideas down! But no, here I am, shooting at bugs and coming up with

Coyote's excuses to the Guardian of Life on why he died."

Moo's toon steps back as the monsters die, pole-arm in hand, and moves to stand next to my character. "Don't listen to them Elo. I like your writing. Let's hear what else you got."

"Pew-pew!" Mythic races across the bridge into the next group, dragging them all to them.

"We can pew-pew and talk!" I follow, sending my ponies in alongside another round of arrows, watching Mags and Moo charge into melee. "Lets see... *look, I almost had him this time. But gravity and a suspiciously placed canyon had other opinions.*"

Mags slams her shield into the bugs. "You know the Road Runner used dark magic, right? His meep-meep is a hex in some ancient dialect."

"Ooh. You might have a point there. He always went meep-meep right before Coyote bit the big one."

"I watched it a lot as a kid. I paid attention to those things."

"I did too, but I never caught on to that one. I got an excuse for the rocks! *I was just testing the boulder's structural integrity with my face. Science y'know.*"

"A lot of rocks did land on him."

"Yep! I even posted a meme in disco a while back, of a boulder in the middle of the road with the caption beneath it. *I bet there is a coyote under that somewhere.*"

"I remember that."

Deacon steps his character up beside Elo. "Are you going to add this to your book? That I stole your shrooms and that I resemble the Coyote?"

"That's a great idea! I might just do that!"

Magnolia laughs. "Don't forget to add that you stole my rook and my bumble bee."

"Mags, Elo needs to make that whole other book!"

"Deacon! How many books do you think I am writing?"

"More than you were. Besides, if you are likening me to Wile E Coyote, that's not fair. Have you seen how fast that bird is? I don't think even rockets can keep up with him."

"Well, they were always faulty anyhow. You would need your Pally pony to keep up."

"Yes, except it doesn't last that long. The Road Runner is like the Energizer Bunny, it keeps going and going."

I groan under my breath. "That's a bad dad joke, Deacon."

"I thought it was quite clever."

"I am NOT adding that!"

"I think you should! Tell them I said it."

"Right. You don't tell readers anything, Deacon. You guide them through a story and hope they like it, unless of course you throw plot twists in that cause emotional damage. One of the raiders sent me a message on disco, asking, why, why, why and a lot of crying emojis. Then he put the emotional damage gif under it all. It's hilarious. I DID warn him he might be mad at me. I can't help it if he didn't heed my warnings!"

"Which book are you traumatizing readers with?"

"*The King's Mystic*. My debut novel."

"Perhaps one day I might read it."

"That will be the day. Just like the day the Coyote actually succeeds at defeating Road Runner. I can see the priestess rolling her eyes at all his excuses."

"Yes, and you know what he would say to that?"

"No, what?"

"He would say... *You said learn from your mistakes, not stop making them. Big difference.*"

"Deacon!"

"What? You know it's true!"

As the last of the oversized bugs crumple to the ground, Mythic charges ahead, his avatar sprinting across the narrow wooden bridge to the next platform. If this wasn't a game, I would swear the bridge would sway ever so slightly under his weight.

The new platform is square-shaped, cobbled with moss-covered stones and flanked by low, gnarled shrubs that have grown wild around its edges, their twisted branches reaching just past knee height of the other players. Well over my toon's head, of course.

Two narrow paths extend from the far side of the platform, though one leads to what looks like a broken connection, an isolated island. The other path continues towards our destination, the end of this dirt and root maze, hanging in the open air.

"Well. If you do actually read it, let me know. I have a secret channel in disco for everyone that has read it."

"Oh, I will."

I shift my toon around the outside, seeing the green acid filling the center, watching as Mythic does his best to kite them around, following me. That's not good. I hate being in melee range. Being a short gnome, I can easily get lost in the fray.

Muttering beneath my breath, I adjust my position and place her safely out on the bridge that goes nowhere. Acid sprays my way and despite trying to move out of the way, I see it strike her and my health plummets.

Clicking on my healing ability, I shift her back a bit more, thinking perhaps choosing a narrow bridge was not the brightest idea. After the sludge disappears, I scoot her towards the platform, circling around the outside, while launching my attacks, deciding that this was a better vantage point.

Deacon thought so too, because he stepped up next to me. "I saw acid hit you, Elo. Did it wreck your outfit?"

"Outfits don't get wrecked, Deacon."

"Then what's a repair button for?"

"Ok, well, the armor does, but no matter how damaged it gets, it doesn't affect the outward appearance. My onesie still looks perfect and lots of people in town comment on how cute it is and ask where they can get it. They can't. It's a limited edition, and it's mine."

"You never know."

"True. Other things are coming back, or versions of them."

"It would be fun though if the outfits deteriorated with the damage they took."

I laugh at the thought. "Some people would be running around naked!"

"Never mind, I retract that thought!"

"I thought you might." I guide my character over the last bridge to solid ground. Almost done. Glancing at the clock, we have more than enough time to see this done. Focusing now, I send in more attacks, clicking the buttons as fast as I can.

# CHAPTER EIGHT

# BIG BAD BUG

"When the last bugs are at fifty percent, I am dragging them into the boss. Haste us then Elo," Mythic comments.

"But the mushroom patch!"

"No time Elo. Timer is too close."

"Got it Mythic." Glancing longingly at the mushroom field, I follow Mythic and the others into the boss' room, watching as he pulls them into the gigantic bug before us. If I thought the ones we were fighting all the way down here were big, this one was the mama bug because she's five times their size.

I circle around, knowing we need to spread out, only to have a gigantic mosquito jump to my character. What the hell? They are not supposed to be in this room. Only the two little bugs and Mama bug.

Now, the game is fun, especially once you get used to playing with certain people. Over time, you learn their patterns; specific words or actions that instantly signal trouble. And honestly, you're usually pretty safe with Mythic. His skills are top-tier, practically legendary. But there's one moment you know things are about to go sideways... when it's too much for even him. When he can't pull us out of trouble.

"Danger. Danger." Mythic murmurs.

Yep, those are the words. The ones you never want to hear when running with him. Anything else and you know he's not worried, even if we feel we are, but those two usually mean we need to run. If we survive long enough.

"We got skeets!"

"Where did they come from?"

"I have no idea. SHIT..." I slam up my shields as five more jump to my character, watching my health plummet and my character die. "Arg! They killed me."

"Sorry Elo, you went down too... What the?"

Seeing his health plummet just as fast as mine. "Deacon! You're not allowed to die in a boss fight."

"Too late Elo. Damn, they do damage faster than I can heal."

"I tried to shield myself. Nada." I pan the screen, watching Mags move around towards our dead bodies, only to see the bugs trounce her, too. "Looks like they are chewing through our group."

"Yep, it does."

Mags mutters, "I was trying to get around to rez you..."

Moo sighs, "I'm down too."

"Right, it's all on Mythic then!"

"This early in the fight? They are killing me, too."

"But Mythic!! You're the powerhouse!"

"Well, power just got disconnected."

Realizing he's dead too, I hit the release button, returning to the rez point at the top of the hill, grateful that I had taken the time to click it.

Calling my pony mount, I charge my character down the slope, knowing the wipe is detrimental to us, and now we are really in a time crunch. Enough so that we might fail this one.

Upon reaching the boss' room, I take the chance and pan around, looking for anything that might indicate where the mosquitoes came from. Nothing. Not on the edges, not in the sky, not on the path we just ran down. Where the hell did they come from? It's like they materialized out of thin air when we pulled the boss. "I don't see any skeets this time."

"Nope, we must have pulled them from elsewhere?"

"But where? We didn't pass any on the way."

"Either way, time is ticking. Let's kill this boss."

"Are we going to make it?"

"Only if you pew-pew!" Mythic wastes no more time and charges in, with Moo and Mags hot on his heels.

Laughing softly, I move my character further into the room, dropping a mark over the boss's head. I scan through my bar, looking for my potions, and click it, making a mental note to buy more in town. Then I click on my haste buff and send Bounce and Downy in.

While working through my rotation, green swirly circles spawn beneath my toon's feet. I move her over, watching as they follow and spin around, trying to catch my character. Shifting her further back, I see they stop and flood outwards, creating a patch of green. Lovely.

Glancing around, I see the same patches surrounding the others. I hope this disappears, because the floor is going to fill up fast. Moving to an empty space, I hear my monitor beeping and look around. Lines cross the room towards Elo and attached to each one is a bug. Even better, baby bugs and they all zero in on my toon.

I scoot her around and head straight for Mythic. First rule of thumb, bring everything to the tank. Once I am in the middle with them, I drop a spell that binds them in place, hoping they get cleaved before they get to me... And that I don't get a second round of them because that spell has a long cooldown on it.

As I reach the outer edge again, I turn, just as purple beams join us all. I race my character away, breaking the beam between us, only to have the green swirly's respawn. Really? Can I not just stand still for a few seconds and attack? At least Moo and Mags downed the baby bugs.

The boss ambles over to a tree and starts chewing on it while large white circles flood the room. I wedge my toon into a small space between them, watching others' health drop as they run over them.

Good thing we have Deacon healing. Speaking of which, I should get my character closer to him. His name is greyed out, meaning I am out of healing range. Turning my screen around, I see him directly across from Elo, and start heading towards him. Only to spot the bugs swarming him. Score, not on my character this time, and that means he's coming to this side of the room.

I focus on the boss, ensuring I use my area attacks to strike the mini bugs too, seeing them drop far faster than the boss. But that's the way it is. Bosses are meant to be tough. Everything beyond the mists is tough, and it's a lesson we are learning today. One that we have learned before but clearly tuned out. Otherwise, we would never step beyond the mists.

Hearing my game tell me more swirls are incoming, I adjust her position over to the clear floor, next to Deacon. Launching a round of arrows, I watch my extra pets charge into the battle. We repeat the process several times, with me side-eyeing the timer. Madly clicking to produce more damage, because we need it.

When the boss finally drops, I glance at the clock, frozen at 31:29 of 31:30.

A gasp escapes me. We did it! With one second to spare. Honestly, I didn't think we would pull it off with how close we were to the time. But we did. I immediately turn my toon to Deacon, and type into the chat. *Elotarra kicks Deacon in the shins. That's for stealing my shrooms.*

Deacon chuckles. "I saw that emote there, Elo. I took your shrooms, and I didn't give a shit."

"Clearly, and that was the point, Deacon. The written word is the only way I can kick your shins and now it's down there forevermore."

"Not sure you want to be kicking that plate armor, Elo. You might break your toes," Mythic replies.

"Nah, it's a game. It will just cost me gold. I will send a bill to Deacon."

"One other thing, Elo... I regretted nothing."

And you know what? I believe him. I can feel Deacon's smile along with the wicked glint in his eyes as he says that.

After staring at the dead body for a moment, each of us breathing a sigh of relief that it's done, we loot the body and part ways, stepping back into the wilds on our own, until fate pulls us together once more.

# Gaming Terms

MMO – Massive Multiplayer Online

DPS – Damage per Second

– Also a nickname for characters that do damage.

Tank – Characters primary roll is to absorb damage

– Also known as a meat shield

Healer – Character that keeps others alive by restoring health with spells

Toons – Nickname for our character online

AOE – Area of Effect

Cleave – Damage that spreads to all the monsters

Dots – Spells that spread to monsters and tick over time

Melee – Fighting up close

Range – Distance between targets or distance of spells limits

Ranged – Fighting at a distance

Aggro – Hostile attention from the enemy

– Usually on the Tank

Trash – Easier groups of monsters to kill

Mobs – Nickname for trash or monsters

Boss – Usually a super tough monster, takes more then one to kill

Addon – Coding that helps with the game, from an outside source

Emotes – Usually something like /cheer and the character will cheer on screen

GM – Guild Master

Guild – A group or club that characters join, each with their own individual names.

Cooldowns – Spells that do extra damage with a longer wait time to recast it

– Aka CD's

– Average cast time is 0-10 seconds. CD's are 1-3 minutes

Logs – Detailed reports of what happens to your character

Buff – Something that adds bonuses to your characters abilities

# Contributors

Cover Design - R Dey.

Beta readers - M Verronneau.

Editor - E McMonnies.

Proofreader - L Horah.

Editing Software - Free Version of ProWritingAid, Google Docs, Impact, Atticus.

Assists - The people that play with me online.

Author Portrait - Gary Woodward.

# Additional Information

T hank you for taking the time to read my stories and I hope that you enjoyed them. If you have, below is a list of my other books. Please feel free to follow me, or add me via Goodreads or Facebook. Also, reviews are important to self published authors, so please take the time to leave one. Thank you.

**Social media** - www.facebook.com/AuthorRandiAnneDey

www.facebook.com/groups/randiswriting

www.goodreads.com/author/show/45347028.Randi_Anne_Dey

**The King's Mystic:** Oct 2023

**The Dragon's Mystic:** May 2024

**Cantara's Mystic:** Apr 2025

**Madison's Web:** Mar 2024

**Dragonscales Divide:** Nov 2024

**Chahaya Durmada: Five Swords of Power:** Eta 2025

**Fae Guardians Poppy**: May 2025

**You Stole my Shroom**: Fall 2025

**Dance, Little Dove: Sept 2025**

**Dating the Damned: Eta 2025**

**Royal Deception:** Tails Scales and Tiaras Anthology  June 2024

**The Emperor's Violet**: Cabs and Crime Anthology  Sept 2025

# About the Author

Randi lives in Victoria, BC. Canada. She is a dog groomer by day and a writer/gamer/reader by night. She partook in the SCA and taught medieval dance for fifteen years. From 2004 until 2022, she attended the Faerie festival annually, keeping fantasy alive in her heart. With multiple books published, she hopes they will draw you away from the modern world and into a land of intrigue and fantasy, where magic, dragons, shifters, fae, vampires and kings roam the lands.